No Wobbly Teeth

First published in 2009
by Wayland

This paperback edition published in 2010

Wayland
338 Euston Road
London NW1 3BH

Wayland Australia
Level 17/207 Kent Street
Sydney, NSW 2000

Series Editor: Louise John
Editor: Katie Powell
Cover design: Paul Cherrill
Design: D.R.ink
Consultant: Shirley Bickler

A CIP catalogue record for this book is available from the British Library.

ISBN 9780750255424 (hbk)
ISBN 9780750255462 (pbk)

Printed in China

Wayland is a division of Hachette Children's Books,
an Hachette Livre UK Company

www.hachettelivre.co.uk

No Wobbly Teeth

Written by Anne Rooney
Illustrated by Fabiano Fiorin

WAYLAND

"Look, Henry! My tooth fell out!" said Henry's sister, Kate.

She put the tooth under her pillow.

The next day, Kate bought
a new hair clip.

"The tooth fairy gave me some money!" she said.

At school, Ben had new
stickers on his lunch box.

"The tooth fairy came," he said.
"I bought these stickers with
the money she gave me!"

Henry really wanted a wobbly tooth.

He poked a tooth with his finger.

No. Not wobbly.
Not even a bit.

"Don't do that, Henry," said Mum. "Your tooth will get wobbly all by itself."

The next day, Lily had
badges on her coat.

"The tooth fairy came!"
she said.

"Did your wobbly tooth hurt?" asked Henry.

"Not much," said Lily.

But Henry's tooth still did not wobble. Not even a bit.

Henry went home. He took
some paper. He drew a tooth.

He cut out the paper tooth
and put it under his pillow.

The next day, the paper tooth was still there.

It was just a bit crumpled.

19

So Henry found a small,
white stone.

He washed it clean. It looked just like a tooth.

He put it under his pillow.

But the stone was still there in the morning.

"What is this stone doing in
your bed, Henry?" asked Dad.

That day, Raheem came to
tea. His mouth looked funny.

"I lost a tooth!" he said.

Henry wrote a note. He put it
under his pillow.

"Dear tooth fairy. Please take
a tooth. Any tooth."

In the morning, all of Henry's
teeth were still there.

None of them was wobbly.
Not even a bit.

Henry went to school.

He didn't look at anyone. He
tried not to open his mouth.

At playtime, Henry bit
into his apple.

Suddenly, he felt
something wobble.

"Look, everyone! I've got a wobbly tooth!" he shouted.

START READING is a series of highly enjoyable books for beginner readers. **The books have been carefully graded to match the Book Bands widely used in schools.** This enables readers to be sure they choose books that match their own reading ability.

Look out for the Band colour on the book in our Start Reading logo.

The Bands are:

Pink Band 1

Red Band 2

Yellow Band 3

Blue Band 4

Green Band 5

Orange Band 6

Turquoise Band 7

Purple Band 8

Gold Band 9

START READING books can be read independently or shared with an adult. They promote the enjoyment of reading through satisfying stories supported by fun illustrations.

Anne Rooney has most of her teeth; none of them is wobbly, not even one. She lives in a state of chaos with her two daughters, a tortoise called Tor2 and a blue lobster called Marcel.

Fabiano Fiorin lives and works in a magical city, Venice, where there are canals full of sea water instead of roads, and there are boats instead of cars. Fabiano thinks the best thing about being an illustrator is that you can pretend to be the characters you draw and you can have lots of adventures.